King of the Birds

Retold by Dawn McMillan

Illustrations by Jenny Mountstephen

Contents

Rigby

HOUGHTON MIFFLIN HARCOURT
Supplemental Publishers

www.Rigby.com
800-531-5015

Chapter 1

Who Shall Be King?

Long ago, the birds of the forest
came together to choose a king.

"We do need a king," said a bright yellow bird,
"but how will we choose him?"

Eagle flapped his huge wings and said,
"We need a strong king.
No bird here is stronger than I am!
I will be King of the Birds."

Owl sat in the hollow tree
and thought and thought.
"Yes, Eagle," she said, "you **are** strong.
But a king needs to be clever, too.
We must have a fair way to decide
who will be king."

"Shall we see how high we can fly?" asked Wren.
"The bird that can fly the highest
must be King of the Birds."

"Good idea!" said Owl.

"Great idea!" said Eagle, laughing.
"None of you can fly higher than I can!"

"Is that so?" asked Wren quietly.

Chapter 2

Flying High

The forest was filled with excitement.
The birds were ready to fly.

Eagle walked back and forth
and back and forth.
He looked at all the birds and boasted,
"Soon I will be your king!
I will be a very fine king, indeed!"

Owl shouted, "**Go!**"
and all the birds flew up into the sky.

Wren flew close to Eagle.
"This is a great place to be," he thought.
"It's easy for me to fly here,
right underneath Eagle,
and he is not able to see me!"

Eagle soared high above the other birds.
One by one, they gave up
and went back to the forest.

"Now I am the only bird in the sky!"
thought Eagle.
And he shouted, "Just look at me!
See how high I can fly!"

Suddenly, the tiny wren darted out
from underneath Eagle
and flew above his head.

"Hello, Eagle," said Wren.
"Look at **me**! See how high **I** can fly!"

Eagle looked up in surprise.
"How can a little bird like you fly higher than a great eagle?" he shouted.

"Oh, Eagle," said Wren, "you are strong, but I am clever!"

Eagle was very angry.
As Wren flew above him,
Eagle reached up and pulled out
the little bird's finest tail feathers.

Chapter 3

Three Cheers for Wren!

Back in the forest, Eagle sat in a tree
and watched the birds gather around Wren.

"We have a new king!" they shouted.
"Wren flew higher than Eagle.
Wren is King of the Birds!
Three cheers for Wren!"

"Yes," said Owl.
"We are happy to have you as our king, Wren.
Eagle wouldn't have been a good king
because he boasts too much."

"Thank you," said Wren. "But look at me!
I have lost my best tail feathers.
Do you really want me to be your king?"

"Yes, please!" shouted the birds.
None of them cared
about the way Wren looked.

And to this day, Wren still has his short tail.
It reminds him of when he flew
higher than Eagle and became King of the Birds.